The
One and Only
Willa Bean

Little Wings

4

The One and Only
Willa Bean

by Cecilia Galante
illustrated by Kristi Valiant

A STEPPING STONE BOOK™

Random House New York

For Jamie, Erin, Catherine, and Hugh,
with love —C.G.

For my One and Only (Psalm 113) —K.V.

Text copyright © 2012 by Cecilia Galante
Cover art and interior illustrations copyright © 2012 by Kristi Valiant

Visit us on the Web!
SteppingStonesBooks.com
randomhouse.com/kids

Educators and librarians, for a variety of teaching tools, visit us at
RHTeachersLibrarians.com

Library of Congress Cataloging-in-Publication Data
Galante, Cecilia.
The one and only Willa Bean / by Cecilia Galante ; illustrated by Kristi Valiant. — 1st ed.
p.   cm. — (Little wings ; 4)
"A Stepping Stone Book."
Summary: Willa Bean thinks that every flying friend should be one of a kind, like her owl, Snooze, and is upset when a new girl arrives at the Cupid Academy with a much larger owl, Mr. Wingston.
ISBN 978-0-375-86950-1 (pbk.) — ISBN 978-0-375-96950-8 (lib. bdg.) — ISBN 978-0-375-98355-9 (ebook)
[1. Individuality—Fiction. 2. Owls—Fiction. 3. Cupid (Roman deity)—Fiction. 4. Schools—Fiction.] I. Valiant, Kristi, ill. II. Title.
PZ7.G12965One 2012
[E]—dc23   2011053001

Printed in the United States of America

10 9 8 7 6 5 4 3 2 1

Contents

Willa Bean's World

Willa Bean Skylight is a cupid. Cupids live in a faraway place called Nimbus, which sits just alongside the North Star, in a tiny pocket of the Milky Way. Nimbus is made up of three white stars and nine clouds, all connected by feather bridges. It has a Cupid Academy, where cupids go to school, a garden cloud, where they grow and store their food, and lots and lots of playgrounds.

Willa Bean lives on Cloud Four with her mother and father, her big sister, Ariel, and her baby brother, Louie. Cloud Four is soft and green. The air around it smells like rain and pineapples. Best of all, Willa Bean's best friend, Harper, also lives on Cloud Four, just a few cloudbumps away.

When cupids are ready, they are given special Earth tasks. That means they have to fly down to Earth to help someone who is having a hard time. Big cupids, like Willa Bean's parents, help Earth grown-ups with things like falling in love. Little cupids, like Willa Bean, help Earth kids if they feel mad, sad, or just plain stuck. Working with Earth people is the most important job a cupid has. It can be hard work, too, but there's nothing that Willa Bean would rather do.

Are you ready for a peek into Willa Bean's world? It's just a few cloudbumps away, so let's go!

Chapter 1

A New Cupid!

"Good-bye, Mama!" Willa Bean waved from the cloudbus window. "Bye, Baby Louie! See you after school!"

"Have fun today!" Mama called. "And take extra-good care of Snooze! Remember, he's never been to the Cupid Academy before!"

Snooze was Willa Bean's flying friend. All cupids were given one before they started the Cupid Academy. Flying friends were from Earth, which meant they knew a lot of things cupids didn't know. When it came time for the cupids to fly down to Earth, their flying friends would go with them.

Snooze gave one of Willa Bean's curls a tug. "You hear that, *ma chérie*?" he asked. "You must take *extra*-good care of me today."

"I always take extra-good care of you, Snooze," Willa Bean said. She gave her little owl an eyelash kiss. "You're my absolute favorite-est."

Harper was sitting next to Willa Bean. "Hey." She gave Willa Bean a little poke. "What about me?"

Willa Bean giggled. Everyone knew that Harper was her best friend in the entire universe. They did everything together, from sharing a seat on the cloudbus to finding cloud treasure all throughout Nimbus.

"You're my favorite *cupid*," Willa Bean said to Harper. "Snooze is my favorite owl."

"I'm your *only* owl," Snooze reminded her.

"That's right." Willa Bean nodded. "Which is another reason why you're my favorite. Onlies are special. Onlies are the best. Everyone knows that." She pulled a piece of cloud treasure from her super-curly hair. "Just like this shell."

"Wolla-wolla-wing-wang!" Harper said. "Where'd you get that, Willa Bean?"

"I found it in my backyard," Willa Bean explained. "Wanna put it in our treasure chest today? After school?"

"YES!" said Harper.

"But you've found lots of shells," said Snooze. "What's so special about this one?"

"It's the only *purple-and-green* shell

I've ever found," Willa Bean told him.

"Ah," said Snooze. "Of course."

"All cupids in their seats, please!" Mr. Bibby called from the front. Mr. Bibby was the cloudbus driver. He was very nice, but he never started the cloudbus until every cupid was sitting down with their cloud-belt fastened.

Willa Bean plopped back in her seat and clicked her cloudbelt. She wiggled her legs and gave Harper's knee a squeeze. "I'm so excited to show Snooze to Class A!" she said. "And I can't wait to meet everyone else's flying friends!"

"Me too." Harper took a bite of a peanut butter Snoogy Bar. "I just hope Octavius doesn't sleep through the whole thing."

Octavius was Harper's flying friend. He was a bat. His favorite thing to do was sleep. He was fond of Snoogy Bars, too, just like Harper. His favorite flavor was oatmeal-raisin.

"Speaking of Octavius," Snooze said, "where is he?"

Harper pointed to her orange cloudsack on the floor. "In there," she said. "Sleeping, of course." Harper lowered her voice. "I think Octavius is a little bit nervous about today. He doesn't like crowds. Are you nervous about today, Snooze?"

"No," Snooze said. "I've been looking forward to today with great anticipation."

"What's ancipitation?" asked Willa Bean.

"An-*ti*-ci-pa-tion," Snooze corrected. "It means that I can hardly wait. I think it will be great fun to meet all the flying friends."

Harper took another bite of her Snoogy Bar. "Octavius is very shy," she said. "I hope he does all right."

5

"I'm sure he will!" said Snooze. "From what Willa Bean has told me about the Cupid Academy, everyone will make him feel most welcome." Snooze blinked his big, round eyes. "Don't you agree, Willa Bean?"

Willa Bean stared straight ahead. She wrinkled her forehead. Then she pushed her bottom lip out, the way she did sometimes when she was thinking hard about something.

"Willa Bean?" Snooze asked. "Did you hear what I said?"

But Willa Bean was not paying attention. "Who *is* that?" she asked instead.

Snooze sighed.

Harper sat forward in her seat. "Who's what?" she asked.

Willa Bean pointed to a new cupid sitting a few seats in front of them. She had small white wings. Her dark hair was twisted into two long braids and tied at each end with a tiny white bow.

"Have you ever seen a cupid with braids like that at the Cupid Academy?" Willa Bean asked.

Harper shook her head.

"Do you think she's in our grade?" Willa Bean whispered.

"I don't know," Harper answered.

"I'm going to ask her," Willa Bean said. She fiddled with her cloudbelt.

"Willa Bean." Snooze tugged at another curl. "Doesn't Mr. Bibby have a rule about staying in your seat while the cloudbus is moving? At all times?"

Mr. Bibby had a lot of rules on the cloudbus. Sitting down before the bus started was Rule #1. Staying in your seat while the cloudbus was moving was Rule #2.

But Rule #3 was that all cupids on the

cloudbus had to be nice to each other. And right now, Willa Bean decided that she was going to follow Rule #3.

"Don't worry, Snooze," she said. "I'll be okay."

When the cloudbus pulled into the next cloudstop, Willa Bean crouched low next to the seats. Then she scuttled down the aisle. In a few seconds, she was at the seat behind the new cupid.

"Hey!" Willa Bean whispered.

The new cupid turned around. "Hi," she said softly.

The new cupid had big blue eyes with long eyelashes. Her hair was very dark and looked soft. When she smiled, her two front teeth stuck out a little in front.

"What's your name?" Willa Bean asked.

"Lucy Summerbreeze," the new cupid answered shyly. "What's yours?"

"I'm Willa Bean!" She lifted the shoulder Snooze was sitting on. "And this is my owl, Snooze."

Snooze made a deep bow. *"Bonjour,* Lucy Summerbreeze," he said. "It is a pleasure to meet you."

Lucy's eyes widened. *"Bonjour?"* she repeated. "What's that mean?"

"It means *hello*," Willa Bean answered. "Snooze is from France. He says a lot of words in French."

"Wow." Lucy gazed at Snooze with wide blue eyes. Willa Bean felt proud. She knew Snooze was going to be a big hit in her class today.

"Is this your first day at the Cupid Academy?" Willa Bean asked.

"Yes." Lucy's voice was soft again. "We just moved to Nimbus. Last week."

"Do you know what class you're in?" Willa Bean pressed. "Because I hope you're in Class A with Miss Twizzle. That's who I have. And Harper, too. We love Miss Twizzle. She's the best teacher in the entire uvinerse."

"U-*ni*-verse," Snooze corrected her.

"That's what I said," Willa Bean said.

"Who's Harper?" Lucy asked.

Willa Bean turned around. She was going to point to where Harper was sitting and tell Lucy that Harper was her best friend. She was going to tell Lucy how their favorite thing to do was to look for cloud treasure. Maybe she would even tell Lucy about their secret treasure chest on Cloud Five. Or maybe she wouldn't. At least, not yet.

But she didn't get a chance to tell Lucy any of these things. Because just then, she heard her name being called from the front of the bus.

"Willa Bean Skylight!" It was Mr. Bibby. He was looking right at Willa Bean in his wide mirror. "What are you doing out of your seat?"

Willa Bean gulped.

"Didn't I tell you?" Snooze whispered. "Now may we go?"

Willa Bean stood up carefully. The rest of the cupids were staring at her. She could feel her face getting hot. "I'm sorry, Mr. Bibby," she said. "I won't get up again."

"Thank you," said Mr. Bibby.

Willa Bean hurried back to her seat.

"Wizzle-dizzle-doodad!" Harper whispered next to her. "You were talking to the new cupid for a long time! What'd you find out?"

Willa Bean looked back at Lucy Summerbreeze.

Lucy gave Willa Bean a tiny wave.

"I think," Willa Bean said, smiling, "that we found a new friend!"

Chapter 2

Fantastic Flying Friends

By nine o'clock, Class A was a sea of cupid wings and flying-friend wings. Willa Bean ran from desk to desk, looking at everyone's flying friend. Sophie had a little black and blue bird. Pedro had a bumblebee. Raymond had a lightning bug. Hannah had a pale orange moth with black dots.

Holy shamoley! They were all wonderful! And so different!

"All right, Class A!" Miss Twizzle stood

up behind her desk as the bell rang. "When the second bell rings, everyone should be in their seats with their wings folded!" She nodded at Willa Bean as she spoke.

Willa Bean rushed back to her desk. Vivi was already sitting in front of her. A large blue butterfly was on top of her red hair. It

had tiny legs, and it opened and closed its wings slowly. It was beautiful.

Vivi was not Willa Bean's favorite cupid in Class A. In fact, Willa Bean was not very crazy about Vivi at all. Vivi liked to tattle on Willa Bean. Plus, Miss Twizzle hardly ever had to tell Vivi twice to do something.

It was hard to sit behind a tattletale who was also a good listener.

Willa Bean slid into her chair and sat still.

"I do hope Miss Twizzle doesn't have to tell you to be in your seat every morning," Snooze whispered in Willa Bean's ear.

"Nope, nope-ity, nope, nope, nope." Willa Bean shook her head. "Hardly ever."

"Now I can make my first special announcement," Miss Twizzle said. "Lucy? Will you stand up, please?"

Willa Bean turned around. With all the flying-friend excitement, she had forgotten about the new cupid from the cloudbus! Lucy was standing behind a desk near the corner. Her cheeks were very pink, and her lower lip wobbled as she tried to smile.

"Class," Miss Twizzle said, "this is Lucy Summerbreeze. Lucy and her family have just moved to Nimbus. I would like all of you to give her a big welcome to Class A."

"WELCOME, LUCY!" Class A shouted.

Lucy smiled. Then she covered her mouth with her hand. Willa Bean wondered if Lucy was embarrassed that her two front teeth stuck out.

"Since it is her first day, Lucy didn't know we were bringing our flying friends to school this morning," Miss Twizzle said. "But a messenger cupid has flown back to Lucy's house to get him."

Willa Bean bounced a little in her chair. She wondered what kind of flying friend Lucy had. Maybe it was a ladybug! Or a blue jay! Maybe it had braids, or little white bows in its wings like Lucy did in her hair! Willa Bean wished she had been able to ask Lucy herself on the cloudbus. One of Willa Bean's favorite things was knowing something no one else did. If only Mr. Bibby hadn't been looking in his mirror!

"And now," said Miss Twizzle, "it's time to introduce our flying friends!"

A murmur sounded throughout the room. Little wings ruffled. Small feet tapped against the floor. Willa Bean hopped up and down in her seat. This was what she had been waiting for!

"Are you ready?" she asked Snooze.

"*Ah, oui,*" Snooze answered. *Oui* was the French word for *yes*. It sounded like *we*.

"*Oui, oui, oui,*" Willa Bean said. She liked speaking French, too.

Willa Bean raised her hand. She waved it back and forth like a flag. She wiggled her fingers and fluttered her wings. She jiggled her feet up and down. "Miss Twizzle!" she yelled. "We're ready, Miss Twizzle! Pick me! Pick me!"

Snooze moved closer to Willa Bean's ear. "Are you supposed to yell and shout like that to get your teacher's attention?" he asked.

Willa Bean stopped yelling. She kept her feet and wings still. "Pleasepleaseplease, Miss Twizzle," she whisper-screamed. "Pick me, please."

But Miss Twizzle did not pick Willa Bean. Instead, she picked Vivi, who was sitting quietly in her seat. The large butterfly with bright blue wings was sitting very quietly, too.

Vivi marched to the front of the room. She stood next to Miss Twizzle's desk, facing the class. Then she reached up and fluttered her fingers. The blue butterfly climbed onto them.

"This is my flying friend." Vivi raised her hand so that everyone could see her butterfly. "Her name is Buttercream Thistlepopper. She is from a place on Earth called Australia."

"HELLO, BUTTERCREAM THISTLEPOP-PER!" Class A said loudly.

"Hello, everyone!" Buttercream Thistle-popper's voice sounded like a soft, high whistle. Her wings were almost as big as Vivi's whole hand.

"She's lovely, Vivi," Miss Twizzle said. "Can you tell us more about her?"

"Well," Vivi said, "Buttercream Thistle-popper is one of the biggest butterflies in Australia. Which makes her a real, live queen of the butterfly kingdom."

Vivi paused. "I just thought of some-thing," she said.

"What's that?" asked Miss Twizzle.

"Well," said Vivi, "since Buttercream Thistlepopper is a real, live queen, don't you think she should be in charge of all the other flying friends?"

Miss Twizzle blinked a few times. Then she cleared her throat. "That is certainly an interesting suggestion, Vivi," she said.

Vivi tossed her long red hair. "Buttercream Thistlepopper is also super-smart," she went on. "She's probably the smartest flying friend that any cupid has ever had. She can *taste* things with her feet."

Class A gasped.

Vivi straightened up taller. "And she can *smell* things with her antennae!"

Class A gasped again.

"*And* she—" Vivi started again.

"Buttercream Thistlepopper is an absolute marvel," Miss Twizzle interrupted gently. "You are lucky to have her. But we have to give everyone a turn to talk about their flying friends. Thank you, Vivi."

Willa Bean stared at Buttercream Thistlepopper as Vivi sat back down. She *was* a beautiful flying friend. And Willa Bean had never heard of any animal being able to smell things with their antennae or taste things with their feet. But she was not too sure about a butterfly— or any other flying friend—telling Snooze what to do.

"Let's hear from Harper next," Miss Twizzle said.

Harper walked up to the front of the class. She gave Willa Bean a little wave.

Willa Bean waved back. "Go, Harper!" she whispered.

Harper turned all the way around until the class could see Octavius. He was hanging upside down from her belt. His eyes were closed. Soft *whee*-ing sounds came out of his nose. He was still sleeping!

"I have a bat." Harper spoke to the chalkboard, since she was turned around. "He likes to hang upside down. And he likes to sleep a lot. Especially during the day. Sometimes he snores."

"A bat!" Miss Twizzle repeated. "How wonderful! Can you tell us anything else about him?"

"He's from a place on Earth called Italy," Harper said.

"Turn around, please, Harper," said Miss Twizzle.

Harper turned around. "He's a horseshoe bat," she went on. "I think it's 'cause his nose looks like a little horseshoe."

"And what's his name?" Miss Twizzle asked.

"Octavius," Harper said.

"*Octopus?*" Pedro whispered behind Willa Bean. "Did she just say Octopus?"

Willa Bean giggled. But she didn't correct Pedro. She didn't want to lose her turn to stand in front of the room. She wanted to tell everyone about Snooze. He was the greatest flying friend ever!

Vivi waved her hand in the air. "Can you wake him up?" she asked. "I want to see the horseshoe on his nose!"

"Harper?" Miss Twizzle asked. "Would it be possible for the class to say hello to Octavius?"

Harper reached behind her and fiddled a little bit until she was holding Octavius. Then she whispered something in his ear.

Class A stared as the tiny animal opened his eyes. He squinted and blinked. "This is Octavius," Harper said softly.

"HELLO, OCTAVIUS!" said Class A.

Octavius's eyes opened very wide. A high-pitched squeaking sound came out of his mouth. Before anyone knew what was happening, he buried his tiny face in the front of Harper's uniform and wrapped his wings around himself.

"What's the matter with him?" Raymond shouted. "Is he going to throw up?"

"No," Harper said. "He's just shy."

"That's perfectly all right," Miss Twizzle

said. "He's here, and that's the most important thing. Thank you very much, Harper. And thank you, Octavius."

Sophie was next. She told the class that her little black and blue bird was a mangrove swallow. He was from Mexico, and he could fly very, very fast. His name was Bobo.

Pedro had a bumblebee named Ranger. He was yellow and black, and when he flew, he made a buzzing sound.

Raymond's flying friend was a lightning bug named Click. Click was from a place called New York City. He had a light on his tail that really worked.

Class A laughed and clapped as Click turned the light off and on. Click was a big hit.

Willa Bean jiggled her knees under her desk while Raymond talked. She tapped her fingers on her desk and tugged on her curls. As soon as Raymond finished, she raised her hand again. She was being very good. Miss Twizzle just had to call her next!

Finally, Miss Twizzle looked at Willa Bean. She smiled and opened her mouth.

But before she could say a word, there was a knock at the door.

Willa Bean stared as Miss Twizzle opened the door. A messenger cupid came into the room with a flying friend sitting on his shoulder.

"Mr. Wingston!" Lucy gasped from the corner. "You're here!"

And with a hoot and a flap of his wings, another brown owl flew across the room.

What Happened to Onlies?

Willa Bean's knees stopped jiggling. She dropped the curl she was tugging. Her mouth fell open into a little O.

She stared at that other owl sitting on Lucy's shoulder. He was twice the size of Snooze. A pair of round silver glasses was settled neatly on his beak. Two tufts of feathers stuck out of the top of his head, like tall ears.

Nope, nope-ity, nope, nope, *nope*! This was not the way things were supposed to go! Not even a little bit! Everyone had to have their own, *completely different* flying friend. No one was supposed to have the same kind! Especially new cupids!

Miss Twizzle looked pleased. "It seems that our special delivery is here! Why don't you go next, Lucy?"

Willa Bean watched as Lucy walked to the front of the class with her owl. The rest of Class A watched, too. Willa Bean wondered if any of them were thinking the same thing she was.

"This is Mr. Wingston." It was hard to hear Lucy, since her voice was so soft. As she spoke, she pulled on the hem of her uniform dress and looked at the floor.

"WELCOME, MR. WINGSTON!" said everyone in Class A.

Well, almost everyone. Willa Bean did not say a word.

"Lucy?" Miss Twizzle asked gently. "I know it's hard, since you don't know anyone yet, but try to speak up, dear. What kind of owl is Mr. Wingston?"

Lucy lifted her head a little bit. "He's a long-eared owl." She pointed to the top of the big owl's head, where his tufts were. "Even though those aren't really ears. They're feathers. But they look like ears. During the day, Mr. Wingston sleeps in my closet."

"Just like me," Snooze whispered in Willa Bean's ear. "How about that?"

Willa Bean wrinkled her nose.

"I love Mr. Wingston's glasses," Miss Twizzle said.

"Thank you." Lucy smiled. "They're called spectacles."

"They make him look very important," Miss Twizzle said. "Which, of course, he

is. Welcome to Class A, Mr. Wingston!"

"Thank you very much," Mr. Wingston replied. He had a low, deep voice. "It's a pleasure to be here."

Willa Bean watched as Lucy walked back to her desk. Mr. Wingston turned his head almost all the way around as he sat on Lucy's shoulder. His yellow eyes blinked behind his silver spectacles. Lucy sat back in her chair. She breathed in deep and let out a big sigh.

Willa Bean knew that wearing spectacles meant Mr. Wingston was super-smart. Harper wore glasses, and she was super-smart-plus! Miss Twizzle had said that Mr. Wingston was very important. Could it be that he was smarter than Snooze?

"Your turn, Willa Bean!" Miss Twizzle said.

Willa Bean did not move.

Snooze nibbled gently on her ear. "Willa Bean," he whispered. "Let's go! It's our turn!"

Willa Bean stood up slowly. She shuffled to the front of the room. She tugged on one of her curls and bit her bottom lip.

"Willa Bean?" Miss Twizzle said softly behind her. "Go ahead, dear. Tell us about your flying friend."

Willa Bean scratched her nose. "I have an owl, too," she mumbled.

Snooze cleared his throat and opened his eyes wide. *"Bonjour!"* he said to the class.

Pedro raised his hand. "What does *bonjour* mean?" he asked.

"Willa Bean?" Miss Twizzle asked. "Can you tell Pedro what *bonjour* means?"

Willa Bean looked at the floor. "It means *hello,*" she said.

"*Yellow?*" Pedro called out. "Did you just say it means *yellow*?"

Miss Twizzle raised her eyebrows. "No shouting out in class, Pedro. Willa Bean said it means *hello*." She clapped her hands together once. "How marvelous!" she said. "Two owls in the same class! I've never had that happen before!"

Willa Bean stared at the floor. She did not think it was marvelous. She wanted Snooze to be the only owl in Class A. Just like Click was the only lightning bug. And Octavius was the only bat. And Buttercream Thistlepopper was the one and only butterfly.

Onlies were special.

Onlies were the best.

Everyone knew that.

"Can you tell us what kind of owl he is?" Miss Twizzle asked.

"He's a pygmy owl," Willa Bean said. "From France. That's why he sometimes speaks French."

"He's absolutely adorable," Miss Twizzle said. "So sweet and tiny! What's his name, Willa Bean?"

"Snooze," Willa Bean mumbled. She wished Miss Twizzle had not mentioned Snooze's size. Especially in front of Mr. Wingston.

"Snooze!" Miss Twizzle repeated. "What a sweet name! Class, can we give Snooze a big Class A welcome?"

"WELCOME, SNOOZE!" shouted all of Class A.

Harper shouted the loudest of all.

"Merci!" Snooze sat up straight. "That means *thank you,*" he added.

"Maybe Snooze and Mr. Wingston can be friends," Miss Twizzle said.

Willa Bean tried to say something, but there was a lump in her throat.

"Thank you for telling us about him, Willa Bean," said Miss Twizzle. "You may take your seat now."

Willa Bean slid into her chair.

"You did not sound very excited about introducing me," Snooze whispered in Willa Bean's ear. "What's the matter?"

Willa Bean shook her head. She did not want to tell Snooze what she was thinking.

In fact, she did not want to think very much right now at all.

Chapter 4

The Flag Flier

"Now that everyone has introduced their flying friends," said Miss Twizzle, "I have one more special announcement."

Willa Bean looked up. She loved Miss Twizzle's special announcements. They were always special. And always fun.

"As you know," Miss Twizzle went on, "we've been working hard all week getting ready for Noble Nimbus Day. Tomorrow is our big celebration, and your parents will come and see all the beautiful things you've been making in class. We'll perform our school song. Afterward, we'll take them to the arena, and you'll show them the lovely twirly-wing dance Mr. Rightflight and I have been teaching you."

"That twirly-wing dance isn't lovely at all," Pedro whispered to Willa Bean. "It's a pain in the wing. I can't remember any of the steps."

Willa Bean giggled. Her inside grumpy feeling was starting to lift a little. She loved the twirly-wing dance. It was almost as much fun as finding cloud treasure.

"Mr. Rightflight and I have been talking," Miss Twizzle went on. "We decided that if your flying friends joined in the dance, too, it might make the show even more special."

Vivi shot up in her seat and held up her hand. "Maybe Buttercream Thistlepopper can *lead* the special twirly-wing dance!"

Miss Twizzle raised an eyebrow. "Mr. Rightflight and I thought the flying friends could all come in at the end of the dance. One of them will be holding the school flag and will fly it to the top of the arena, while the rest will form the letter *N,* for *Nimbus.* It will be a perfect finish to the celebration."

Class A cheered.

"Whew," said Snooze softly. "For a minute there, I thought I was going to have to learn how to dance."

Willa Bean giggled.

Miss Twizzle clapped her hands. "I'm glad you're excited," she said.

Vivi raised her hand again. "Miss Twizzle, can Buttercream Thistlepopper hold the flag? Since she's a queen?"

Miss Twizzle tapped the side of her

cheek. "I don't think that will work, Vivi," she said. "We're going to need a larger flying friend to hold the flag. It's a little heavy." Miss Twizzle's eyes swept the room. "Mr. Wingston will do perfectly. Mr. Wingston, would you do the honors?"

Lucy's eyes were wide. She stared at Mr. Wingston and held her breath.

Mr. Wingston stuck out his wing and

bowed deeply. "It would be an absolute pleasure," he said.

Lucy beamed.

But Willa Bean's heart quivered.

She forgot about the twirly-wing dance. She forgot about Noble Nimbus Day. She put her head down on the desk.

"Willa Bean?" Snooze gave her ear a little nibble. "What's wrong, *ma chérie*? Don't you feel good?"

"No," she whispered back. "I have a stomachache."

"Do you want me to tell Miss Twizzle?" Snooze asked.

Willa Bean shook her head.

"Now that everything is settled," said Miss Twizzle, "let's line up for music class. We need to practice that school song!"

Snooze sat quietly on Willa Bean's shoulder as the cupids lined up at the door.

Harper scooted in behind Willa Bean. She gave one of Willa Bean's purple wings with the silver tips a little tug.

"Ouch!" said Willa Bean crossly.

"What's the matter?" Harper whispered. "You look un-Snoogy-ish."

Willa Bean frowned. "What does *un-Snoogy-ish* mean?"

"Well, Snoogy Bars make me happy," Harper explained. "And when I don't have one, I'm sad. Which means that when I'm sad, I'm un-Snoogy-ish."

"Oh," Willa Bean said.

Snooze shook his head. "I'm dizzy," he said.

"Are you worried that your talk about Snooze didn't go well?" Harper asked. "'Cause I thought you did great! Everyone loved Snooze!"

"No." Willa Bean poked the floor with

her big toe. "I'm not worried about that."

"Are you tired?" asked Harper.

"No," Willa Bean said.

"She has a stomachache," Snooze said.

"You have a stomachache?" repeated Harper.

"No," said Willa Bean. "I don't have a stomachache."

"You just told me you had a stomach-ache," Snooze said.

"Well, I did," Willa Bean answered. "But now I don't anymore."

"I'm dizzy again," said Snooze.

Just then, they heard Miss Twizzle up front. "Lucy? Mr. Wingston? Could you come to the front of the line? That way, I can show you around as we go to music class."

Willa Bean watched Lucy and Mr. Wingston go to the front of the line.

"Hi, Lucy!" said Harper.

Lucy gave Harper a little smile.

She gave Willa Bean a wave.

Willa Bean waved back. Just a little.

And then she turned around again, folded her arms, and pushed out her bottom lip.

A School Song

One by one, the cupids filed into the music room. Harper and Willa Bean sat in the second row by Hannah and Sophie.

"Why don't you sit there for now, Lucy?" Mr. Sunhorn, the music teacher, pointed to the empty seat next to Willa Bean.

Lucy sat down next to Willa Bean. Mr. Wingston perched on the chair in front of her.

"Good morning, cupids!" Mr. Sunhorn

looked all around the room. "And good morning to all of your flying friends! My, what a diverse group of animals we have in here today!"

Raymond raised his hand. "What's *diverse*?"

"It means all different kinds," Mr. Sunhorn explained. "So many originals! How wonderful!"

Vivi raised her hand. "Actually, Mr. Sunhorn, there are two owls," she said. "Snooze *and* Mr. Wingston."

Willa Bean stared at the back of Vivi's head. What would happen if she reached out and yanked Vivi's hair? She would get into trouble, that's what. Big Trouble. With a capital *B. T.* And not just at school. But back home, with Mama and Daddy, too.

"Hmph," Willa Bean said instead. She pushed out her bottom lip again.

"I'm very excited that your flying friends have agreed to be part of our Noble Nimbus Day show." Mr. Sunhorn tapped his long silver stick on the edge of his desk. "We have lots of work to do. Let's start by going over our school song."

Class A groaned.

"I know we've spent a lot of time on it already," said Mr. Sunhorn. "But some of you keep forgetting the lines. This is your school song, cupids. It's important that you know it forward and backward. You should be able to sing it in your sleep."

"My little brother yells in his sleep," said Pedro. "Then he flies around the room until he bumps into something, and my mom has to come put him back in his bed."

Mr. Sunhorn's lips twitched. "Thank you for sharing, Pedro," he said.

He handed Lucy a piece of paper. "Since this is Lucy's first day, she can use the sheet music to follow along. Everyone else must try to remember the words. Sit up straight, please."

The cupids sat up straight. Willa Bean looked around nervously. She hoped she wasn't the only one who still didn't know all the words to the song.

"Wings back!" said Mr. Sunhorn.

Willa Bean straightened out her little wings.

"Chins up!" said Mr. Sunhorn. He sat down at the piano. "All right now, cupids, sing out!"

Willa Bean tried to sing the Cupid Academy song. It went like this:

The sun is warm.
The moon is bright.

In here, we learn
What's wrong and right.
This is our school.
It's only one.
But every day,
We have such fun.

Willa Bean knew the first part of the song by heart. It was the second part that gave her trouble. She just could not re-member all the words.

Harper didn't seem to be having any trouble. And on her other side, Lucy and Mr. Wingston were singing, too. Willa Bean tried not to look at the words on Lucy's sheet music, but it was hard. It was so close!

Mr. Sunhorn lifted his hands off the piano. "Eyes straight ahead, Willa Bean. Only Lucy may look at the sheet music."

Willa Bean felt her cheeks get hot.

Snooze cleared his throat. "Willa Bean," he whispered into her ear, "I don't know it, either. Just do your best for now. We can practice together later."

"You don't *have* to know it." Willa Bean's grumpy feeling was getting worse. "Only I do."

Harper gave Willa Bean a little nudge. "I keep forgetting some of the lines, too," she whispered. "Don't worry. We'll go over it on the bus."

"One more time!" said Mr. Sunhorn. "From the beginning, please!"

Class A started again. Willa Bean sang, too. "The sun is warm. The moon is bright. . . ."

Suddenly, Mr. Sunhorn stopped playing again. "Where is that marvelously deep baritone coming from?"

"What's a baritone?" asked Pedro.

"It's a very low male singing voice," explained Mr. Sunhorn. He looked at Mr. Wingston on the chair in front of Lucy. "Is that you, Mr. Wingston?"

Mr. Wingston straightened his spectacles with one wing. "It could be," he said. "I've been told I have a very deep voice."

"Can you sing the first two lines?" Mr. Sunhorn asked. "Just by yourself?"

Mr. Wingston sat up straighter and ruffled his chest feathers. "The sun is warm," he rumbled. "The moon is bright."

Lucy beamed.

"Oh, bravo!" Mr. Sunhorn clapped loudly. "What a voice! Mr. Wingston, promise me that you will sing extra loud on Noble Nimbus Day. I want everyone to hear that beautiful baritone of yours!"

"With pleasure," said Mr. Wingston.

Willa Bean watched as Lucy petted Mr. Wingston's long ear tufts. She watched as she gave him a squeeze and then an eyelash kiss.

It wasn't fair. Snooze had a wonderful voice, too, but Mr. Sunhorn had only said something to Mr. Wingston.

Maybe Willa Bean had spoken too soon about that stomachache of hers.

It was back again. And now it wasn't just her stomach.

She had a headache. And a wing-ache.

And maybe even a heartache, too.

Chapter 6

The Letter N

Willa Bean felt a little bit better when the time came for the cupids to practice their twirly-wing dance. Dancing made her happy. And doing the twirly-wing dance made her even happier.

She got in line behind Harper and tried not to wiggle.

"Line up against the wall, cupids!" Mr. Rightflight blew his silver whistle as the cupids filed into the arena. Mr. Rightflight was the flying teacher at the Cupid Academy. He had red wings and not much hair. When he wanted to get the cupids' attention, he blew the silver whistle around his neck.

Willa Bean's stomach did a little flip-flop when she heard Mr. Rightflight's whistle. She was crazy about that silver whistle. It was bright and shiny and loud, too. It was super-treasure-plus.

"First of all, I'd like to welcome all the flying friends!" Mr. Rightflight walked back and forth as he talked. "Having them here will add a lot of excitement to our Noble Nimbus Day celebration."

Class A cheered.

Willa Bean jumped up and down.

Miss Twizzle beamed.

"Wizzle-dizzle-doodad!" said Harper. "It's going to be the best Noble Nimbus Day ever!"

"Wonderful," said Mr. Rightflight. "Now, flying friends gather over here, next to Miss Twizzle, please."

Harper took Octavius out of her cloud-sack. "I know you're nervous," she whispered, "but you have to go with everyone else, little buddy."

Octavius yawned. He looked around the big arena, but he didn't move a wing.

"He can come with me." Snooze put a wing around the little bat. "Stay close,

Octavius. We'll do this together." He flew off with Octavius at his side. Mr. Wingston followed. Soon they had joined the other flying friends next to Miss Twizzle.

Mr. Rightflight walked back and forth in front of the flying friends. "Now, Miss Twizzle has told me that the long-eared owl is going to be our flag flier," he said.

Mr. Wingston took a step forward. He straightened the spectacles on top of his beak. "At your service," he said.

"After Mr. Wingston comes in with the flag," said Mr. Rightflight, "the other flying friends are going to follow. They will be holding beautiful purple scarves and will spell out the letter *N,* for *Nimbus,* in the air. We need to practice a few times, of course, so let's line up now from biggest to smallest. Buttercream Thistlepopper, let's start with you. Your wings are enormous!"

Vivi beamed as her butterfly scooted in behind Mr. Wingston.

"After that, we'll have Octavius," Mr. Rightflight said.

Octavius gave a squeak and hid behind Snooze.

Mr. Rightflight read off a list of flying-friend names. "And then Bobo, Click, Ranger, and finally Snooze," he finished.

Willa Bean stood up. "But, Mr. Rightflight!" she shouted. "You said biggest to smallest! Snooze isn't the smallest! Why is he last?"

Mr. Rightflight closed his eyes.

"Willa Bean!" Miss Twizzle called gently. "If you have a question for Mr. Rightflight, please raise your hand."

Willa Bean sat back down on the bench. She twisted a curl around her finger and gave it a good yank. Was she the only one who saw how unfair things were?

Mr. Rightflight opened his eyes again. "I think this will work out quite nicely, Willa Bean," he said.

Harper leaned in next to Willa Bean. "I hope Octavius does all right. Group activities make him nervous."

"Don't worry," Vivi said loudly. "My flying friend will take care of everyone. She's a queen. That's her *job*."

Mr. Rightflight's whistle sounded.

Willa Bean jumped.

"Oh!" said Lucy. She clapped her hand over her mouth. Her blue eyes were very wide. They followed Mr. Wingston as he flew through the air. Willa Bean watched, too. The big owl soared to the top of the arena. He held the purple-and-white flag in his claws. It fluttered and flapped as he turned and hovered high in the air.

"Beautiful!" shouted Mr. Rightflight. "Now the others, please!"

Slowly, the rest of the flying friends followed.

Buttercream Thistlepopper.

Octavius.

Another flying friend.

Then a couple more.

Bobo was next.

Then Click.

And Ranger.

And finally, Snooze.

"I need Bobo and Click to stretch their wings out a little more!" said Mr. Rightflight. "That's right! Terrific! Hold it there!"

The animals hovered, floating above Mr. Wingston in the shape of a giant N. Their purple silk scarves fluttered out beneath them.

"YAY!" Sophie shouted.

"You look gorgeous, Buttercream!" Vivi shrieked.

"Awesome, Click!" shouted Raymond. "You're doing great!"

"Don't be nervous, Octavius!" Harper yelled. "And try not to fall asleep!"

Lucy gave Willa Bean a nudge. Her eyes were shining. "Don't they look great?" she whispered.

Willa Bean stared up at the flying friends.

Mr. Wingston looked great. Buttercream Thistlepopper looked great.

Octavius looked nervous, but great, too.

The other flying friends all looked great.

But Ranger's purple scarf kept blowing in front of Snooze.

In fact, Willa Bean thought as her eyes began to fill with tears, she could hardly even see her little owl at all.

Chapter 7

Species Queasy

That night at dinner, Willa Bean made a big mountain out of her peas. She had already scooped out the middle of her mashed potatoes. It looked like a lake. A piece of carrot stuck out of the middle of it. It was a carrot-fish.

"What's the matter, Willa Bean?" Mama asked. "You've hardly eaten a thing tonight. Aren't you excited about your big day tomorrow?"

Willa Bean kept making a mountain

out of her peas. "Yes." She sighed. "I'm very excited."

"Noble Nimbus Day!" Daddy said. "With all your flying friends! You certainly don't sound very excited."

"It's just that I don't understand something," Willa Bean said. "You told me that all the cupids get *different* flying friends."

"They do," said Mama, shoveling a spoonful of peas into Baby Louie's mouth.

"Goo!" Baby Louie stuck a pea into his nose.

"Every cupid always gets a completely different animal," Daddy said. "That's how it works."

"But that's not what happened today," Willa Bean said. "Lucy Summerbreeze has an owl, too. Just like me."

"Who's Lucy Summerbreeze?" asked Ariel.

Ariel was Willa Bean's sister. She was in one of the older-cupid classes. Sometimes she could be a real pain in the wing.

"She's new," Willa Bean answered. "She came today. And she has an owl, just like Snooze."

"*Exactly* like Snooze?" Daddy asked.

Willa Bean nodded.

"Lucy's owl is a pygmy owl?" Daddy pressed. "From France?"

"Well, no." Willa Bean piled some more peas on top of her pea-mountain. It was getting super-high. "Her owl is a long-eared owl. He wears glasses. I forget where he's from."

"Well, there you have it!" Daddy said. "You don't have the same flying friend at all. Long-eared owls are as different from pygmy owls as humans are from cupids."

"But I'm supposed to have the *only*

owl," Willa Bean said. "All the other cupids have onlies. Raymond has the only lightning bug. Harper has the only bat. Even Meany-Mouth Vivi has the only butterfly." She sniffled back tears. "It's not fair! I'm the only one without an only!"

Ariel rolled her eyes. "Willa Bean, there

are only so many flying animals in the world, you know. It's not that big a deal that someone else has a different kind of owl. Don't be a baby."

"Ariel," Daddy warned, "be kind to your sister, please. And, Willa Bean, I do not want to hear you calling anyone in your class a 'meany-mouth.' Remember the Cupid Rule."

Willa Bean stared down at her pea-mountain. The Cupid Rule went like this:

The very best way
To spend your day
Is to try to be kind—
All the time.

It was a short rule. But it was hard to follow. In fact, sometimes it felt like one of the hardest rules of all.

Daddy patted Willa Bean's hand. "Ariel is right about one thing, little love. There just aren't enough flying animals to go around. Sometimes cupids have different species of the same animal."

"What's a species?" Willa Bean asked.

"It's just a type of animal," Daddy said. "Like elf owls and spotted owls and long-eared owls and pygmy owls. So none of them are really the same at all."

Willa Bean rolled another pea onto her mountain. She stared sadly as it rolled off and slid to the other side of her plate. She didn't understand what Daddy was talking about. Not even a little bit.

Besides, what did species have to do with onlies?

Nothing, that's what.

Nothing at all.

After dinner, Snooze and Willa Bean took a pajama flight. The sky was a soft blue with a little bit of gray underneath, and the sun was almost gone. Willa Bean flew ahead, trying to think.

It was hard.

She had a lot on her mind.

Mostly about onlies.

And Snooze. And Mr. Wingston, too.

"Willa Bean?" Snooze called from behind. "What's the matter? You haven't been yourself all day."

Willa Bean shook her head. How could she tell Snooze that she felt bad that he wasn't an only anymore? And how could she tell him that she was worried because Mr. Wingston was bigger—and maybe even better at owl things—than he was? She did not want to hurt Snooze's feelings. Not even a little bit.

"Willa Bean?" Snooze said again. "Don't you want to tell me?"

Willa Bean shook her head.

"I think you're a little nervous about tomorrow," Snooze said, flying in close.

"There will be a lot going on. Maybe you're feeling overwhelmed."

"What does *overwhelmed* mean?" asked Willa Bean.

"It means that something feels like a lot," Snooze answered. "Maybe too much at the moment." He tugged on one of Willa Bean's curls. "But remember, *ma chérie*. No matter how overwhelmed you feel, I'll be with you the whole time. Right next to you."

Willa Bean leaned in and gave her little owl an eyelash kiss.

She knew how lucky she was to have a flying friend like Snooze.

But for the first time in her life, she wished he was a little bit bigger.

And that he wore spectacles, too.

Chapter 8

Noble Nimbus Day!

"Good-bye, Mama!" Willa Bean waved from her seat as the cloudbus pulled away. "Good-bye, Baby Louie!"

"Good-bye, sweetheart!" Mama called. "Good-bye, Snooze! We'll see you both in a little while!"

"*Au revoir!*" Snooze adjusted the black hat he was wearing. It was called a beret and was from France. Snooze liked to get fancy on special occasions.

Then Snooze looked at Willa Bean.

"What are you doing, Willa Bean?"

"Looking at myself." Willa Bean stared at herself in the cloudbus window. "I want to look beautiful for Noble Nimbus Day. And especially for the twirly-wing dance."

"You look sensational," said Harper.

"Thank you." Willa Bean patted her hair on the right. She patted her hair on the left. She pushed it down on top and tried to squish it flat. Mama had tried the same thing that morning. But her hair only boinged out again. Well, she just couldn't help it. Her hair had a mind of its own.

Next, she stood up and smoothed down the front of her uniform. Mama had ironed it that morning, so there were no wrinkles. Plus, it was very clean. Willa Bean had found a few cloud treasures on the way to the cloudstop. She had put them in her hair instead of her pockets so that her

uniform wouldn't get dirty. Now she just had to try to keep it clean.

Suddenly she heard her name being called. Her long name. The one Mama used when she was not pleased with something Willa Bean was doing.

"Wilhelmina Bernadina Skylight!" Mr. Bibby called from the front of the bus. "Sit *down*, please!"

Willa Bean sank down into her seat. She could feel Mr. Bibby watching her in his rearview mirror as he brought the cloud-bus to a stop.

"I'd like to talk to you for a moment, Willa Bean," Mr. Bibby said. "Please come up here."

"Wizzle-dizzle-doodad!" Harper stared at Willa Bean. "Take a deep breath, Willa Bean!"

"Let's go, *ma chérie*." Snooze fluttered his wings.

Willa Bean walked slowly up to the front of the bus. Everyone was watching her. She pulled at the hem of her uniform and took a deep breath.

"That's a very sharp bow tie you have on today, Mr. Bibby," she said. "Red is definitely your color."

Mr. Bibby straightened his bow tie. "I

take my job as a cloudbus driver very seriously, Willa Bean," he said. "And I have rules on this bus for a reason." He tugged gently on one of Willa Bean's curls. "There is only one of you, Willa Bean Skylight. And I want you to be safe, to make sure it stays that way."

"All right," Willa Bean whispered. "I'll try harder, Mr. Bibby."

"Thank you." Mr. Bibby turned back around. "Take your seat now. Miss Twizzle is not going to be pleased if I bring her cupids in late for Noble Nimbus Day."

The sound of buzzing and fluttering and flapping and hooting filled the room as Willa Bean, Harper, and Lucy walked into Class A.

"Maybe Octavius isn't the only one who's nervous," Harper said. She pointed at something across the room. "Look!"

Willa Bean looked. Vivi was jumping up and down and reaching with her arms. Above her, Buttercream Thistlepopper flew in circles. Once, twice, a third time. "Come down, Buttercream!" Vivi shrieked. "It's all right! Just come down!"

"Hoo boy," said Snooze. "I have a feeling today is going to be a very long day."

"You can say that again," said Mr. Wingston.

Harper hurried to her desk. "It's almost time for the bell," she said. "And I want to give Octavius a little pep talk before we start."

"If you can wake him up," said Willa Bean.

"Yes." Harper sighed. "If I can wake him up."

Willa Bean sat at her desk with Snooze.

She watched as Vivi got her butterfly to come back down. Then she straightened Snooze's hat. "You look handsome, Snooze," she said.

"*Merci,*" said Snooze. "Good luck today, Willa Bean."

"*Merci,*" said Willa Bean. "You too." She snuck a peek in Lucy's direction. Lucy was smoothing Mr. Wingston's ear tufts and straightening his spectacles. She didn't seem worried because Mr. Wingston wasn't the only owl in the room. But maybe that was because Mr. Wingston had so many important things to do.

Snooze didn't have anything important to do. Not even a little bit.

"All right, cupids!" Miss Twizzle said. "I know everyone is excited, but we have to settle down! Parents are already starting to come into the building."

A murmur swept through Class A.

Willa Bean's knees hopped up and down under her desk.

"We'll bring them in here so they can see your artwork first," said Miss Twizzle. "Then we'll sing our class song for them and take them to the arena for our big finale!" She clapped her hands together once. "Is everyone ready?"

"YES!" shouted Class A.

"Are all the flying friends ready?" Miss Twizzle asked.

"YES!" shouted all the flying friends.

"Oui!" shouted Snooze.

"Wonderful!" Miss Twizzle's cheeks were turning pink. "Let's make this a Noble Nimbus Day to remember!"

Chapter 9

A Secret Screech

Willa Bean waved wildly as Mama, Daddy, and Baby Louie came through the classroom door. They were in line with the rest of the cupid parents. Mama looked especially beautiful. She had curled her long blond hair and put on a golden necklace.

"Over here, Mama!" shouted Willa Bean. "Here I am, Daddy!"

Daddy waved.

Mama smiled and put a finger against her lips.

"Willa Bean," Snooze warned.

"I know, I know." Willa Bean wiggled back down in her seat. "I'm just wriggly!"

The next hour went quickly. Willa Bean showed Mama, Daddy, and even Baby Louie all the drawings she had done that year. It took a long time. There were a million-bajillion of them.

"What's that one, little love?" Daddy asked.

"That's me and Harper," said Willa Bean. "We're looking for cloud treasure."

"Ah," said Daddy.

"Your drawings are beautiful," Mama said. "And so detailed! I love the piece of cloud treasure in Harper's hand."

Willa Bean wrinkled her nose. "That's not cloud treasure!" she said. "That's a Snoogy Bar!"

"Bah!" shouted Baby Louie.

"Oh," said Mama. "Of course."

After artwork, it was time for the cupids to sing their school song. Mama, Daddy, and Baby Louie followed the rest of the parents into Mr. Sunhorn's music room. They sat down in chairs, while the cupids stood in the front of the room.

Willa Bean felt fluttery inside. She hoped she wouldn't forget any of the words.

Harper squeezed Willa Bean's hand. Willa Bean squeezed her hand back.

"Is everyone ready?" Mr. Sunhorn raised his silver stick in the air. Then he looked at Mr. Wingston, who was perched on top of the piano. "Mr. Wingston, are you ready to sing?"

The owl nodded.

The cupids began to sing. "The sun is warm. The moon is bright. In here, we learn what's wrong and right. . . ."

Willa Bean's nerves began to jump and wiggle. This was the part she had a hard time remembering. "This is our school. It's one and one. And every day, we run and run!"

Willa Bean looked around. Had she messed it up? She couldn't remember.

The parents clapped and cheered. Willa Bean smiled happily. The parents wouldn't be clapping and cheering if she hadn't gotten the words right. It had sounded wonderful!

"Willa Bean," Mama said afterward, "you sounded marvelous, sweetie! And who was that owl up front with the beautiful voice?"

Willa Bean's happy feeling began to fizzle. "That's Mr. Wingston," she said.

"What a voice!" Daddy said. "A true baritone, I think!"

Willa Bean pushed out her bottom lip. Who cared about dumb old singing voices? And who cared about dumb old owls with weird ears that stuck out of the tops of their heads? Everyone knew real owls didn't have ears like that!

But Mr. Wingston was a big owl. He was smart and important. Miss Twizzle had even said so. And now Mama and Daddy thought he was wonderful, too.

"It's time for our grand finale!" Miss Twizzle called out. "If you will please follow me to the arena, our cupids *and* our flying friends have a big surprise for you!"

Everyone hurried after Miss Twizzle.

Everyone except Willa Bean.

"Willa Bean?" Snooze looked puzzled. "Let's go. You don't want to be late for your dance. And I have to get ready for the flag flying."

"I don't want to go." Willa Bean poked at the floor with her toe.

"Why not?" asked Snooze.

"Because you look silly," Willa Bean said. And then she burst into tears.

"I look *silly*?" Snooze repeated. He took off his tiny hat. "Is it my hat? I don't have to wear my hat."

Willa Bean shook her head. She had already said too much. She did not want to say any more.

"Willa Bean," Snooze said after a moment. "We have to go. Silly or not, we don't want to let Miss Twizzle down."

Willa Bean nodded. And she followed Snooze to the arena.

"What's the matter?" Pedro asked as he began the twirly-wing dance with Willa Bean. "Were you crying?"

Pedro was Willa Bean's dance partner. He was not a very good dancer. He stepped on Willa Bean's toes a lot.

Willa Bean shook her head. "It's nothing," she said.

Pedro and Willa Bean took two steps to the right. Then they took two steps to the left.

"Ow," Willa Bean said as Pedro stepped on her foot.

"Sorry," said Pedro.

Harper was across from Willa Bean. She was dancing with Raymond. Vivi was paired up with Sebastian, and Sophie and Hannah danced together. Lucy sat with her parents. There hadn't been enough time for her to learn the dance. Still, she smiled as she watched. She looked happy.

"Ready to twirl?" Pedro whispered.

Willa Bean nodded. She lifted her

purple wings with the silver tips and twirled straight up into the air. She twirled and twirled and twirled. Usually, this was Willa Bean's most favorite part of the twirly-wing dance. But right now, it did not feel very fun. In fact, her wings felt like bricks. She had just told Snooze that he looked silly. And she did not know how she could take it back.

Finally, the dance was over. The parents cheered and shouted as the cupids took their bow. Willa Bean smiled a little bit as she saw Baby Louie jump up and down in Mama's lap.

Harper grabbed Willa Bean's hand. "Come on!" she said. "Let's go sit over here, so we don't miss any of the grand finale!"

Willa Bean sat down next to Harper. She felt nervous inside again, just as she had in the music room. Everyone would shout and yell when they saw Mr. Wingston fly out with the flag. But no one would be able to see Snooze, especially if Ranger's purple scarf got in the way.

Mr. Rightflight's silver whistle sounded. Willa Bean and Harper jumped.

"Oooooooh!" said all the cupid parents as Mr. Wingston appeared.

The big owl swooped into the arena. His ear tufts streamed back against his head, and his eyes were wide and yellow. The purple-and-white flag fluttered behind him.

"Aaaaahhhhhh!" said all the parents as Buttercream Thistlepopper appeared next. Her scarf streamed behind her in a wave of purple silk.

The other flying friends flew in next, holding their scarves, and finally Snooze came last.

The parents oooohed and aaaahed some more as the flying friends formed the letter *N*. It was a good letter *N*. Big and straight. Right over Mr. Wingston.

Snooze held his scarf perfectly and stayed in place, just as Mr. Rightflight had said he should. But it was hard to see him, especially when Ranger's scarf flapped up and down.

Suddenly, up above, there was a commotion. Something—or someone—was falling.

"Golly-wolly-wing-wang!" Harper cried, getting to her feet. "It's Octavius! I think he fell asleep!"

Willa Bean jumped up, too. She watched as Mr. Wingston flew down toward the floor and snapped the big flag out straight. Snooze was flying, too, toward the falling shape. What was happening?

Miss Twizzle gasped.

The cupid parents rose to their feet.

Mr. Rightflight blew his silver whistle.

But Snooze and Mr. Wingston seemed to be the only ones who knew what to do. Quick as a flash, Snooze caught the other end of the big flag in his beak. And then, as Mr. Wingston pulled his side, the two owls brought it under the falling bat until—

PLOP! Octavius fell into the middle of the flag.

"Octavius!" Harper rushed over. Willa Bean followed. So did Lucy.

Harper cradled the little bat in her arms. He opened one eye slowly. "Oh, Octavius! What happened?"

"I don't know," the bat answered with a squeak. "I was just so sleepy. And we were up so high. And there were so many people."

Harper squeezed her bat close. Lucy put her arm around Mr. Wingston.

"You saved Octavius!" Pedro said, looking at Mr. Wingston.

"Actually," Mr. Wingston said, "I didn't even notice until Snooze gave me an alarm hoot."

"An alarm hoot?" Willa Bean repeated. "What's that?"

"It's a screech sound that owls make," Snooze said. "When someone's in trouble."

"Only owls can hear it," Mr. Wingston said, nodding. "It's a good thing both of us were here. Otherwise, who knows what might have happened?"

Willa Bean sat on the floor next to Snooze and pulled him into her lap. She petted his soft head feathers. "You gave Mr. Wingston an alarm hoot?" she asked softly.

"I did, indeed," answered Snooze. "How else was I going to let him know that Octavius was in trouble?"

"You're a very smart owl." Willa Bean's voice quivered a little.

"*Merci,*" said Snooze.

"And very sweet, too," she added.

"*Merci* again," Snooze said.

And that was all Willa Bean could say.

Because a lump in her throat made it too hard to say the rest.

It would have to wait until later.

Chapter 10

Onward, Onlies!

The ride home on the cloudbus was noisy. All of the cupids were talking at the same time. They were still buzzing about everything that had happened on Noble Nimbus Day.

Only Willa Bean was quiet, maybe for the first time in a very long time. She was thinking. Mostly about what Mr. Wingston had said earlier, about both owls being there to help Octavius. She was thinking, too, about how Mr. Bibby had said there was only one of her. Maybe there was more to onlies than she had thought. Maybe she had gotten it all wrong.

Snooze was quiet, too. But he was not thinking. He was snoozing inside Willa Bean's cloudsack. The day's activities had pooped him out.

Slowly, Willa Bean unzipped her cloudsack. "Snooze?" she whispered.

Snooze opened one eye. "Yes?"

"I'm really sorry I said you looked silly," Willa Bean said. "I didn't mean it. I wanted you to be an only, and then I got so mad when you weren't."

Snooze opened his other eye. "But I *am* an only," he said. "Don't you see? There will always be other owls, but there is only one Snooze. And *that* makes me an only. Just like there will always be other cupids, but only one you."

Willa Bean scooped her little owl out of her cloudsack. She held him close and gave him an eyelash kiss. Lucy might have the biggest flying friend. Harper might have the sleepiest. But Willa Bean's flying friend was the sweetest one. She was sure of it.

The cupids talked even more loudly.

"I can't believe owls have their own screeches!" Harper said. "Golly-wolly-wing-wang!"

"And when they swooped down and saved Octavius, that was the coolest!" said Pedro. He stretched out his arms, pretending to swoop down like an owl.

"My favorite part was when Buttercream did her little somersault at the end." Vivi flipped her hair over her shoulder. "But that's 'cause she's a queen."

"Then Mr. Wingston and Snooze should be kings!" Raymond said.

The rest of the cupids laughed.

Lucy smiled. Her cheeks turned pink. She covered her mouth with her hands.

Willa Bean raised her hand. "Mr. Bibby?" she called.

Mr. Bibby looked in the mirror. "Yes, Willa Bean?"

"Can Harper and I move our seat?" Willa Bean asked. "Just for a minute?"

"You must wait until we stop at the

next cloud," Mr. Bibby said. "Then you may move your seats. And thank you for asking, Willa Bean."

"What are you up to?" Snooze asked.

Willa Bean straightened Snooze's hat. "You'll see."

When the cloudbus stopped at the next cloud, Willa Bean and Harper sat behind Lucy. Mr. Wingston was on her shoulder, watching something out the window.

Lucy turned around. Willa Bean had flutters in her stomach. And a little bit of nervous wiggles in her knees.

"Hi, Willa Bean," Lucy said softly. "Hi, Harper. Did you have fun today?"

Willa Bean nodded. She swallowed hard, hoping it would help the wiggles go away. "I almost didn't, though," she said.

"Because of the accident?" Lucy looked worried.

"No." Willa Bean shook her head.

"Then what?" Lucy asked.

"I was kind of mad," Willa Bean said. "That you had an owl. And that he was bigger than Snooze. And maybe better, too."

Mr. Wingston turned his head slowly. He blinked his eyes once. And then again. "Me?" he asked. "Better than Snooze? But that's impossible."

"I know," Willa Bean said. "You're both owls. And you're both onlies."

"Onlies?" Mr. Wingston cocked his head.

"Yes!" Willa Bean looked at Lucy. "And you're an only, too, Lucy!"

"I am?" Lucy asked.

Willa Bean pointed. "Because of your braids! And your cute teeth!"

Lucy blushed. She covered her mouth again.

But Willa Bean shook her head. "Nope, nope-ity, nope, nope, nope!" she said. "It's more fun to be different. Look!" She turned around and wiggled her wings. "I have purple wings with silver tips! And a million-bajillion curls!"

"And I love sweet stuff!" Harper said. "I could eat a whole barrel full of Snoogy Bars! In one night!"

"I have marvelous vision," said Snooze. "And a special fondness for French things."

"I have feathers that look like ears," said Mr. Wingston. "And a very sharp pair of spectacles."

"I wear funny bow ties!" Mr. Bibby called out from the front of the bus.

"Mr. Bibby!" Willa Bean laughed. "You were listening in!"

Slowly, Lucy uncovered her mouth. "I guess I'm a little shy," she said softly. She

smiled a little and stuck out her hands. "And I'm new, too."

Harper took one of Lucy's hands.

And Willa Bean took the other.

"You're not new anymore!" said Willa Bean. "After today, you are definitely a Noble Nimbus cupid!"

Lucy beamed.

And this time, she did not cover her mouth.

Don't miss out on

Willa Bean's

other wacky adventures!

Little Wings
1
Willa Bean's
Cloud Dreams
by Cecilia Galante
illustrated by Kristi Valiant

978-0-375-86947-1

Little Wings
2
Be Brave, Willa Bean!
Galante
Kristi Valiant

978-0-375-86948-8

Little Wings
3
Star-Bubble Trouble
by Cecilia Galante
illustrated by Kristi Valiant

978-0-375-86949-5

Illustration © 2011 by Kristi Valiant